Early Step into Reading™

The Berenstain Bears
RIDE THE
THUNDERBOLT

Stan & Jan Berenstain

Random House 🏠 New York

The Thunderbolt!

Waiting in line.

Buying tickets.

Getting on.

Buckling up.

Going up.

Up, up, up!

Clickety-clickety

clackety-click!

At the top.

Going down.
Down, down, down!
Clackety-clackety
clickety-clack!

Down and around!

Upside down!

Into the dark!

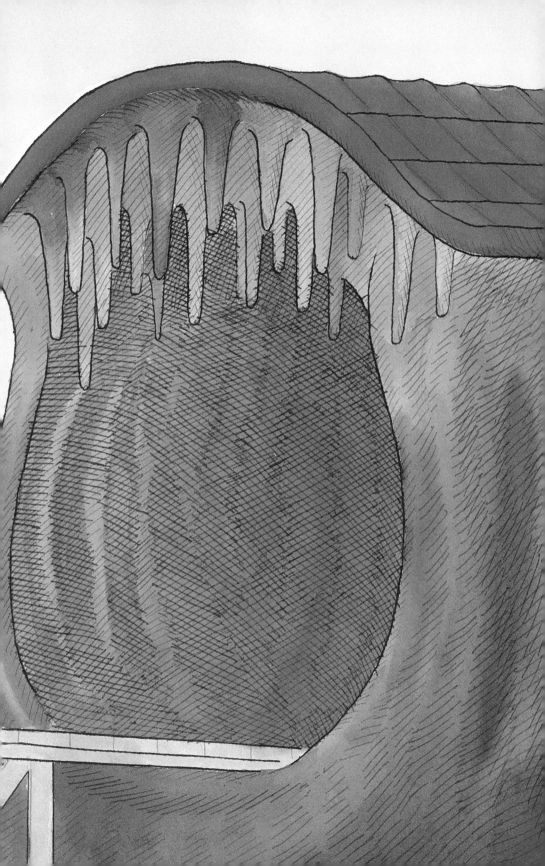

Into the light.

Slowing down.

Getting off.

"Again! Again! Do it again!"

"Not so quick!
Not so quick!
Your papa looks
a little sick."

"But that was fun!
That was fun!"

Going on again,
minus one.